Detective LaRue
Letters from the Investigation

Written and Illustrated by
Mark Teague

Scholastic Press New York

The Snort City Regi

September 30

For Lillias and Ava

Library of Congress Cataloging-in-Publication Data:
Teague, Mark.
Detective LaRue : letters from the investigation / by Mark Teague.—1st ed.   p. cm.
Summary: While on vacation, Mrs. LaRue receives letters from her dog Ike who has
been falsely accused of harming the neighbor's cats and is trying to clear his name.
ISBN 0-439-45868-4
[1. Dogs—Fiction. 2. Cats—Fiction. 3. Letters—Fiction. 4. Humorous stories.] I. Title.
PZ7.T2193825 Dg 2004   [E]—dc22   2003020082

10 9 8 7 6 5 4 3 2 1   04 05 06 07 08
Printed in Singapore 46   First edition, September 2004

The display type was set in American Typewriter Bold. The text type was set in 14-point
ITC American Typewriter Medium and 18-point Litterbox. The illustrations were painted
in acrylics. Book design by Mark Teague and David Saylor

HIBBINS' CATS MISSING

Dog Suspected

In a possible case of feline foul play, two Snort City cats were reported missing yesterday, and hours later a neighborhood dog was captured by police.

Although there was no sign of forced entry, the cats were apparently abducted from their Second Avenue apartment.

"I simply can't imagine them leaving on their own," said owner Leona Hibbins. "My darlings wouldn't dream of upsetting me like that."

Supporting Mrs. Hibbins' theory was the capture in Gruber Park of local dog Ike LaRue, whom police described as "suspicious." LaRue was apprehended while attempting to bury a bag of cat treats.

"Ike has always had it in for my cats," said Mrs. Hibbins, citing an altercation on the building's fire escape two winters ago ("Police Blotter," January 16). "I just want to know what he did to them this time."

The dog's owner, Gertrude R. LaRue, is currently vacationing in Europe.

Ike will be detained at police head-quarters pending further investigation.

Police nab LaRue

October 1

Dear Mrs. LaRue,

I hate to disrupt your vacation, but you must return immediately! An unfortunate misunderstanding (as well as very sloppy police work) has landed me in jail. The case involves the Hibbins' cats, who have mysteriously disappeared. As usual, everyone blames the dog, without even considering whether the cats might be guilty of something. (Needless to say, reports that I was attempting to "steal" their strangely yummy cat treats are entirely false!) Come home now!

Sincerely,
Ike

P.S. This must seem sadly familiar.

Dear Mrs. LaRue,   October 2

The police continue to interrogate me about what happened to
the Hibbins' cats. I wish I knew! The last I saw of them, they
were sunbathing in Gruber Park. I went to retrieve their cat
treats (which they had foolishly left by the swings) and when
I returned, they were gone.
    I know Mrs. Hibbins is upset, but I'm sure she'll get over it.
Between you and me, they weren't very good cats.

Sincerely,
Ike

P.S. Imagine how I feel cooped up inside this loathsome
dungeon!

October 3

Dear Mrs. LaRue,

If you really want to know why I was in Gruber Park, the truth is that I was doing Mrs. Hibbins a favor. The cats had threatened to damage her apartment (as only cats can) unless I let them out for some "fresh air." Reluctantly, I agreed. Now it appears they had more in mind than a simple walk in the park. My kindness was repaid with deception. I have learned my lesson.

Regretfully yours,
Ike

P.S. No, I do not think it would be "best" for me to remain with the "nice police" until you finish your vacation!

October 4

Dear Mrs. LaRue,

I can't begin to tell you how dire this situation has become! Mrs. Hibbins insists that I am responsible for losing her cats. Plus, she has managed to convince everybody that they were rare and valuable. Nobody stops to consider how unlikely that is!

But nothing is being done to find them! Apparently it is easier for some people to blame a dog than to solve a crime. In fact, the police claim to be working on another case entirely! It looks like I will have to take matters into my own paws and solve this mystery myself.

Your intrepid dog,
Ike

P.S. Besides, it has become shockingly apparent that you do not intend to come get me.

The Snort City Register/Gazette

RECORD PUMPKIN AWARDED AT FAIR

TURNIP ALSO HONORED

RECORD PUMPKIN

EEC RULES
STILL LO[...]
[...] TODAY

MORE CANARIES STOLEN

THE HOUND OF THE BASKERVILLES

The Snort City Register/Gazette

October 5

LaRUE FLEES CUSTODY

Cats Still Missing

Just days after being captured, local dog Ike LaRue apparently escaped from police headquarters yesterday. "He just sort of walked out," admitted Officer Louis "Sparky" Waldorf. LaRue is considered a suspect in the earlier disappearance of two cats belonging to Leona Hibbins of Second Avenue. Waldorf acknowledges that the investigation into that case has stalled. "We've all been distracted by the canary burglaries. Until we can establish who has been stealing these birds, I'm afraid we won't be able to focus on the Hibbins' cats." (For more on the canaries, see page A1.) As for LaRue, Waldorf speculated that the dog will return "as soon as he gets hungry."

CANARY BURGLARS STRIKE AGAIN!

Snort City Police report that two canaries and a mynah bird were stolen from the Birdland Pet Store on Flopworth Street last night. The burglary closely resembles thefts from other stores this week, and may mark the beginning of a major crime spree. Investigators admit to being completely baffled. "We can't figure out who would commit such crimes," said Chief Detective Mavis Bickle.

October 6 — South Snort City

Dear Mrs. LaRue,

Yes, I have escaped. Furthermore my search for the Hibbins' cats has taken me into an awful part of town. Here cats roam the streets freely, day and night, howling, knocking over trash cans, and clawing people's ankles as they walk by. It's a terrible place, Mrs. LaRue, but by handing out a few cat treats I've been able to turn up some very interesting facts. For instance, did you know that cats regularly capture and eat small animals? I had no idea.

I will tell you more as the case begins to unfold.

Sincerely,
Ike

P.S. Imagine the danger and hardship!

SNORT CITY
Plaza
HOTEL

October 7 — South Snort City

Dear Mrs. LaRue,

Today my investigation led me to a pigeon named Rocco who told me that half his family was lost in attacks by—you guessed it!—cats. It seems that even our lovely feathered friends are not safe from these little monsters. It's clear to me that I must find Mrs. Hibbins' cats quickly—for the good of the city!

Yours truly,
Ike

October 8 — Trundlebrook

Dear Mrs. LaRue,

I followed a tip up here to the Trundlebrook Cattery. I wanted to find out if "valuable" cats behave any better than the little brutes I've been seeing downtown. Clearly they do not! In fact, I was told that the ONLY way to keep small animals safe is to keep cats inside!

Sincerely,
Ike

Dear Mrs. LaRue,

October 9 — Back in Snort City

The news today is all about the latest canary burglary. Only this time, the criminals made off with two parrots and a gerbil as well. Have you noticed that this terrible crime wave began just after the Hibbins' cats disappeared? It isn't a pleasant thought but, of course, a dog must follow his instincts.

Yours,
Ike

The Snort City Register/Gazette

CANARY BURGLARS STRIKE

The Snort City

CANARY BURGL STRI

LARUE STILL AT LARGE

Dear Mrs. LaRue,

October 10 — From an Undisclosed Location

Welcome home! I wish I could be there to greet you properly but, as you know, I am "on the lam." Until I can solve this case I must remain in hiding. It is a situation rife with intrigue and danger. As I close in on the culprits, the police remain intent on catching me! Unfortunately they have no idea who the real criminals are. As long as they continue to regard the cats as innocent victims, they'll be "barking up the wrong tree." Perhaps I can think of some way to tip them off.

Your sleuth,
Ike

October 11

Gruber Park, Outside the Small Pet Emporium

Dear Mrs. LaRue,

Just this morning, I discovered that the very first canary burglary was here—on the night of my arrest! Apparently the sneaky villains climbed the fire escape at the Small Pet Emporium and made off with six plump birds. To think that I was the unwitting pawn in their wicked scheme! But I've heard that criminals always return to the scene of the crime and, if that's true, I have a feeling the Hibbins' cats will be here shortly. I just called the police.

Wait! I think I see them up on the fire escape! Gotta go!

Ike

The Snort City Register/Gazette

October 12

CATS RESCUED!
LaRue Saves Day

Responding to an anonymous tip, Snort City police rushed last night to the Small Pet Emporium, where they were able to assist hero dog Ike LaRue in his rescue of two lost cats. The cats, beloved pets of local resident Leona Hibbins, had been missing for twelve days. Though clearly traumatized by their ordeal, they appeared healthy and very well fed. LaRue apparently found the cats clinging to a fire escape and was able to hold them until police arrived. "To tell the truth, we had considered the dog a suspect, especially after he escaped," said Chief Detective Mavis Bickle. "We see now that he was simply determined to save his little friends."

"He was searching for the cats all week," confirmed the dog's owner, Gertrude R. LaRue, who recently returned from France. "I'm proud of my Ike."

Even Mrs. Hibbins, who had been critical of LaRue prior to the rescue, was full of praise. "I completely misjudged him," she admits. "I never knew he cared so much about my cats."

Lucky cats happy to be rescued by police

October 12 — Police Headquarters

Dear Mrs. LaRue,

Unfortunately you can't believe everything you read in the newspaper, though they portrayed my own heroism nicely. I'm afraid the police completely misjudged the situation. Instead of making an arrest, they made a "rescue"! Oh, well. Somehow humans are never able to see the truth about cats. For me, that's the real mystery.

Anyway, the police are a swell bunch. I have no more hard feelings about what happened.

See you soon,
Ike

The Snort City Register/Gazette

October 20

LaRUE NAMED HONORARY DETECTIVE
Dog Praised in Police Ceremony

In a ceremony at City Hall yesterday, local dog Ike LaRue was presented with a detective's badge and was cheered wildly for his role in rescuing two cats earlier this month. "What he did there was first-rate police work," said Chief Detective Mavis Bickle. "I'm sure he'll be a credit to the force." The ceremony was made possible by an almost complete absence of crime over the last few days. "Even the canary burglaries seem to have ended," said Bickle. "We've had a lot of free time on our hands." (See story page A2.)

Mayor Mitzy Slepper agreed. "Nothing else is happening," she said. "It seemed like a good time for a ceremony."

When asked what duties Ike LaRue might be expected to perform, Detective Bickle smiled. "If he keeps an eye on those wonderful cats," she said, "that'll be enough for us."

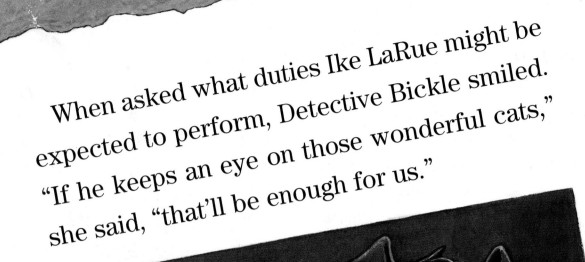

Grateful cats embrace their hero